# Quentin Blake
# SIMPKIN

**RED FOX**

SIMPKIN
A RED FOX BOOK 978 1 849 41676 4

First published in Great Britain by Jonathan Cape,
an imprint of Random House Children's Books

Jonathan Cape edition published 1993
Red Fox edition published 1995

7 9 10 8

Copyright © Quentin Blake, 1993

The right of Quentin Blake
to be identified as the author and illustrator of this work
has been asserted in accordance with the Copyright, Designs and Patents Act 1988.

RANDOM HOUSE CHILDREN'S BOOKS
61–63 Uxbridge Road, London W5 5SA
A division of The Random House Group Ltd

Addresses for companies within The Random House Group Limited can be found at:
www.randomhouse.co.uk/offices.htm

THE RANDOM HOUSE GROUP Limited Reg. No. 954009

A CIP catalogue record for this book is available from the British Library.

Printed in China

# Here is
# SIMPKIN

Simpkin
ONCE

and Simpkin
TWICE

# Simpkin NASTY

# Simpkin NICE

# Simpkin FAST

and Simpkin SLOW

Simpkin HIGH

and Simpkin
LOW

Simpkin
ROUND and ROUND
the chairs

Simpkin UP

and DOWN the stairs

# Simpkin THIN

and Simpkin FAT

Simpkin THIS

and Simpkin THAT

Simpkin WEAK

and Simpkin STRONG

Simpkin SHORT

# and Simpkin LONG

# Simpkin SMOOTH

# and Simpkin ROUGH

and Simpkin
THAT IS QUITE ENOUGH

Simpkin WARM

and Simpkin CHILLY

Simpkin SENSIBLE

and

SILLY

And

sometimes

when

we

stand

and

call

Simpkin

JUST

NOT

THERE

AT

ALL